The Ghost of Mingo Creek and other spooky Oklahoma Legends

Greg Rodgers

foreword by Tim Tingle

Forty-Sixth Star Press
Oklahoma City
2008

Copyright © 2008 by Forty-Sixth Star Press

All rights reserved. No part of this book may be reproduced in any form or by any electronic or mechanical means, including information storage and retrieval systems, without permission in writing from the publisher, except by a reviewer who may quote brief passages in a review.

First Edition

Cataloging-in-publication Data

Rodgers, Greg, 1968-
The ghost of Mingo Creek : and other spooky Oklahoma legends / Greg Rodgers ; foreword by Tim Tingle ; [edited by Larry Johnson]
104 p. : ill. ; 21 cm.
Summary: A collection of short stories based on spooky Oklahoma legends.
ISBN-13: 978-0-9817105-0-1 (alk. paper)
ISBN-10: 0-9817105-0-1 (alk. paper)
1. Legends--Oklahoma. 2. Folklore--Oklahoma.
3. Tales--Oklahoma. 4. Short stories.
I. Johnson, Larry, 1966- ed. II. Title.
GR110.O35 R63 2008
398.209766--dc22

Conceived, written and printed in the forty-sixth state of the union

Printed in the United States of America

www.fortysixthstarpress.com

CONTENTS

- 9 The Ghost of Mingo Creek
- 23 Mr. Apple's Grave
- 33 Jimmie the Doodlebug
- 48 The Boy Who Cried Lion
- 59 Deadman's Treasure
- 69 The Kiamichi Bigfoot
- 79 The Red River Monster Fish
- 88 The Witch of Kitchen Lake

dedication

The author would like to dedicate this book to Malachie, Lexi, Cameron, Stevie, and Dylan – the little rays of goodness that brighten even the darkest days.

ACKNOWLEDGEMENTS

Appreciation for a project like this runs back a lifetime and can never possibly include all the folks that have inspired the words, or the crafting of the words. But the biggies include: Tim Tingle, mentor and friend, Pam and Buddy, publishers/editors extraordinaire, and, of course, my family, whose support and encouragement seems, oft-times, simply heroic.

The publisher would like to express her appreciation to Linda T. Bracken for her generous support in this endeavor and for her continuing support of arts and culture in Oklahoma. My thanks to Nell for her keen eye and patience. Finally, as always, Jandy was there every step of the way.

Foreword

When another talented and driven writer emerges from the good red dirt, it is a time to celebrate. Well folks, pull out your fiddles and rosin up your bows. In his debut, Greg Rodgers offers eight eerie tales for the middle reader, tales of headless ghosts seeking ill-gotten gold, fiery witches, graves guarded by rattlesnakes, and even a guest appearance by Oklahoma's most beloved backwoods creature, Bigfoot himself.

However, Bigfoot, witches, and monsters notwithstanding, in this book written for children, the children steal the show. Siblings rival and reconnect, little sisters rescue big brothers, and paperboys peddle furiously from "glowing yellow eyes."

The Ghost of Mingo Creek presents fictional renditions of our state's lore in well-crafted narratives peopled with recognizable Oklahoma characters. Affable oilmen of a bygone era strut and fret with sod-dwelling loners. Among my favorites are the Wilkerson brothers, "the worst fishermen ever." They are loveable, laughable blue-collar deities, and we know them well. We see them every day at the gas pump and convenience store.

Mingo Creek offers enjoyable reading for all ages. For teachers, parents, and librarians seeking new ways to stimulate student interest in Oklahoma history, geography, and social patterns, these stories will prove to be a valuable tool.

They can be read simply for the joyride of a well-told tale. But take note of the book you hold. A keen mind has created a collection of subtle gems that glow as hidden treasure. As a special bonus, eerie black-and-white photographs perfectly frame the unique world and tone of every story.

Greg Rodgers is a storyteller, performing often on elementary campuses, and thus understands grade-level appropriateness. He knows how to usher the young listener, now the reader, into that deep and elusive cavern of the story. From the spoken word to the written page, *The Ghost of Mingo Creek* delivers in a book that crackles, slithers, jumps, and always hits the mark.

Tim Tingle

The Ghost of Mingo Creek

Tulsa was first settled by peoples of the Muscogee Creek Nation following the Trail of Tears in the 1830s. First called Tullasi, meaning "Old Town," by its earliest inhabitants, Tulsa would remain little more than a trading post along the Arkansas River until the railroad came in 1882. Within just a few years, the town would boast a population of several thousand. Oil was discovered across the river in 1901 and by the 1920s, the city grew to well over a hundred thousand residents. But there was a time in those early years—before the oil booms — when simple folks farmed the rich black soil of the Arkansas River Valley. The following is just one of the stories those folks used to tell...

Back before Oklahoma became a state, Carrie Jewett lived near Owasso in Indian Territory. The Jewett family had settled on two plots of land along the banks of Mingo Creek. Carrie's older brother David farmed the section of land next to Carrie's, also bordered by the creek. Though she had heard the old stories meant to frighten children into behaving, Carrie never believed in ghosts. Not really. Not until that summer night in 1896 when she saw one.

Carrie was walking through her pasture after feeding the horses. The sun had set and the evening sky was holding its last bit of light from the fading day. As she walked past the hay barn, once an old log home, she saw a glow through the doorway of the crumbling structure. Inside was the dark outline of a man holding a lantern. *Must be a drifter looking for a bit of shelter,* she thought, and kept walking.

Early the next morning, she awoke thinking of the stranger in her barn and worrying that his lantern might catch the hay on fire. She dressed and made her way to the barn. It was undisturbed. There were no signs of the stranger at all. Soon, the events of the night before drifted further from Carrie's mind.

That evening she saw the man walking across the pasture and holding his lantern in front of him. There was something not quite right about how the lantern illuminated his body. It seemed lopsided. Carrie felt a cold chill run down the base of her neck. As the man came toward her, he lifted the lantern higher and Carrie realized what made the man appear so oddly shaped – the stranger had no head.

Frozen with fear, she could only stare as the headless ghost walked past her and disappeared into the creeping gloom of the trees beyond the pasture. When Carrie could move again, she hurried home, deciding to tell no one what she had seen.

Two nights passed with no more sightings of the specter. David appeared on the morning of the third day, entered the house and eased into his favorite old rocking chair. After a long moment of silence, he raised his eyes to meet his sister's.

"I got somethin' to tell ya, if you promise you won't laugh at me," he started.

"I won't," she said.

"I was feeding my hogs last night when a man came walking right through the whole mess of 'em. I got real spooked. By the way he moved – like he was floating just off the ground – I knew something weren't right. And you know me, Sis. I would fight the devil himself and give him the first lick, but all I could do was just stand there, slack-jawed, like a thunderstruck polecat. And Carrie…he didn't have no head."

"I know," said Carrie. "I saw him, too, and I was so scared I couldn't move."

"I know what you mean," her brother said. "I ain't been so scared since I was nine years old and that old bull of grandpa's got loose and chased me halfway to China."

"Did you see where he went?" Carrie asked.

"Who? The bull?"

"No, Noodle-head. Not the bull, the ghost. Did you see where the ghost went?"

"I sure did. He went down to the creek and then just disappeared."

"I wonder who he was and most of all, I wonder what he wants," Carrie pondered. "He must be lookin' for something, the way he carries that lantern around."

"Maybe he's looking for his head."

"Maybe he wants one of our heads," said Carrie.

"Well, he ain't gettin' mine," said David, "and yours neither if I can help it."

"You better help it. I kinda like my head just where it is and I'd like to keep it."

"Don't worry, Sis. I'll keep ya safe."

Sunday morning they went to church together, and Carrie became concerned when she did not see Mrs. Pelzer, her German neighbor. Carrie asked around, but no one had an answer for her friend's mysterious absence. After church, Carrie and her brother stopped by the Pelzer home. Mrs. Pelzer and her husband had six boys and three girls. Between all the chores that needed doing and the playful chaos of children on the move, their home was usually hopping with activity. Stepping onto the porch of the two-story farmhouse, it struck Carrie how quiet the place was. *Where is everyone*, she wondered. The eerie silence sent chills up Carrie's spine.

"Mrs. Pelzer!" Carrie cried out. "Anybody home?"

David pushed on the front door. It creaked slowly open. With a nod from Carrie, he stepped through the doorway.

"The coals in the fireplace are still warm," said David.

Carrie made her way down the hallway. As she neared the room she knew to be Mrs. Pelzer's, she heard a small whimper coming from behind the door. It sounded like a wounded puppy. Carrie knew the Pelzer's didn't have a dog. She thought of waiting for David, but if her friend was in the room, she might be in danger. Carrie drew in a deep breath and entered. There was Mrs. Pelzer, slumped against the wall next to her armoire. Without lifting her head, she began to scream.

"Go away! Leave me be!"

"Mrs. Pelzer! It's me – it's Carrie Jewett."

The older woman lifted her eyes, slowly. Her face was white with fear.

"Carrie? Oh…dear…you gave me such fright. I sought you vas dat headless man come to get me."

Carrie gently lifted Mrs. Pelzer to her feet and led her to the kitchen table. Warming a pot of coffee, Carrie listened as her neighbor recounted her own horrifying experience.

"I vas milking mein cows ven I saw a headless ghost-man mit a big light standing at the gate. I vas so scared, I dropped the milk bucket and ran to the house."

"Here drink this. It will help," said Carrie, handing her friend a warm cup.

"Oh!" said Mrs. Pelzer, "I forgot to close the gate. The cows vill be in the corn by now.

"I'll take care of it," said David.

"Danke, dat is so kind."

"Did the ghost talk to you?" asked Carrie.

Mrs. Pelzer sipped her coffee and shook her head. The color in her face was returning to normal.

"Where are Mr. Pelzer and the kids?"

"Day vent to the town for some things we need. The plow blade is broke and my husband took it to be fixed. He even took dat new hired man to help, leaving me here all alone. I am so glad you came by here."

"What new hired man?"

"Oh, the really strong man that come last veek. Mr. Pelzer needed help to bring in the harvest so he hired this stranger mit the big shoulders. Mort something."

"Why don't you go lay down, Mrs. Pelzer?" Carrie said. "David and I will stay with you till your husband gets home."

Several days later, David and Carrie returned to their neighbor's home. Mr. Pelzer, a burly man of forty-three, offered David a seat on the porch while Carrie went inside to see Mrs. Pelzer.

"Now, David," began Mr. Pelzer, "I was thinkin' about this ghost we got walking around the creek and I figure he's lookin' for something. I think I know what it is. Before you and Carrie came to live here, there was a man lived up at that old log home Carrie uses as a barn. He pretty much kept to himself, but one day old Henry Masters said he heard the man talking to himself about burying money he had robbed from some bank back east.

"Later, someone found the old man down by the creek without no head. Folks figured his gang had come looking for the money. When they didn't find it, they kilt him. Now I'm thinkin' that ghost must be the old man come back to find his loot."

"It makes as good a'sense as anything else, I reckon," said David.

"I figure if we hide nearby, the ghost'll lead us to his buried money."

At that exact moment, the Pelzer's new hired hand, Mordechi Luggs, came walking around the corner of the house. He was carrying a scythe across his shoulders and was covered head-to-toe in sweat and sticky bits of grass.

"Did I hear something about buried money?" he asked.

David and Mr. Pelzer looked at each other and said nothing. David shrugged his shoulders and Mr. Pelzer motioned for Mordechi to take a seat on the front steps. "I guess we could use some help digging."

Mordechi settled on the top step and lifted his straw hat, revealing tangles of glistening golden hair. He wiped his brow and twisted and turned till his deep-set eyes locked on the two older men.

Glancing toward the front door, Mr. Pelzer leaned forward and lowered his voice.

"I guess you probably heard about the ghost walking along the creek at night?"

"Yep, I sure did," answered Mordechi.

"Well, we figure that old ghoul is looking for some lost money he buried and we aim to get it for ourselves. We're gonna dig along the creek where we've seen him."

"I think I can save some time in that regard," said Mordechi. "My pappy was a diviner down in Georgia. He could take a forked branch from a peach tree – one struck by lightning – and use it to find water and just about anything in the ground. I noticed one of your own peach trees out back was lightnin'-struck. I figure I seen my pappy do it so many times that surely I can, too."

Again the two exchanged looks. David shrugged and then nodded.

The smile on Mordechi Luggs' face spread and his eyes became narrow slits of dark ambition. He stood, swatting at the flies that hovered above his head. "I'll go find us the right peach sprig and meet you fellas back here about sundown."

David stood and said, "I'll go get my shovel and pick axe." Then he hollered into the house. "C'mon Carrie, we're leaving."

Carrie stepped from the house, wiping her hands with her white cotton apron.

"We got lots to do tonight," said David, "and I gotta get back here as quick as I can. I'll tell you all about it on the way home." They stepped from the porch and headed down the road.

"I don't like it," said Carrie. "Even if you find the money, what makes you think the ghost will let you keep it? And what do you plan to do with this money if you find it?"

"Well, I always fancied a new suit and a shiny black carriage," he said.

"You should think some more on this, David Jewett. It would be bad luck to keep any money that comes from other folks' hurts and miseries."

"Don't you worry none, Sis. Everything's gonna be just fine."

Below the creek embankment, David, Mr. Pelzer, and Mordechi waited undercover in the gloom of late night darkness. The creek bed curved sharply, reaching deep into the fields near Carrie's barn. Bats flitted by as they chased mosquitoes and mayflies in the moonlight. The wind shifted and the night-time air took on the smell of death.

"There he is," Pelzer whispered.

The ghost stood above them, the lantern rocking in his bony grasp. The three men crouched below the bank and held their breaths. The thin, gold-green light of the lantern cast an eerie glow along the creek bed. In the blink of a moment the embankment was again shrouded in darkness. It took a minute for the men to readjust to the once-more black of night. David peered slowly, first with one eye and then the other, over the earthen wall.

"He's gone," he whispered. The other two peeked over and looked for themselves.

"He was plain as day," said Mordechi. "Then he was just gone."

"The money must be close by," said David. Pelzer nodded.

The three men scrambled atop the embankment. Mordechi held the forked peach sprig in front of him. With his hands on the branches and the main stem pointing outward, he walked in an ever-tightening circle. The closer to the center he came, the more the branch twitched and jerked.

As he tightened his turns, the convulsions spread to his arms and chest. A loud humming filled the air and Mordechi struggled to keep his grasp on the branch. David and Mr. Pelzer covered their ears from the deafening sound. Finally, Mordechi fell to his knees and thrust the end of the branch deep into the earth.

The humming stopped.

"It's here," Mordechi said, collapsing on his back and gasping for air. David rushed to him and helped him to his feet.

"I think we've done enough for tonight," Mr. Pelzer said. "We'll come back when its daylight."

The next morning, long before light settled on the rooftops, David joined Mr. Pelzer, who said, "Let's get Mordechi and go start digging."

"Right behind ya, buddy," said David, slapping the older man on his shoulder.

As the two approached the hired hand's sleeping quarters, Mr. Pelzer hollered, "C'mon, Mordechi. Rise and shine, boy. Today is the day the Lord hath made. Let's rejoice in it."

Mr. Pelzer opened the door to an empty room. Even the blankets were gone.

"The money!" David shouted. Both men took off running for the creek.

They located the place where they had stood just a few hours earlier. Instead of the forked branch stuck in the ground, they found a mound of fresh dirt – a big empty hole.

"Mordechi," growled Mr. Pelzer. "That rotten sneak thief."

Three hours later, after saddling their horses and riding several miles on either side of the creek, David and Mr. Pelzer gave up looking for any sign of Mordechi's tracks. The thief was long gone and there were no clues to follow.

Twenty miles to the southeast, Mordechi Luggs slept in the cold, wet confines of a prickly vine, afraid to light a fire. A distant howling sound woke him in a fright shortly after midnight. He rose to his knees and looked around.

"It's only the wind," he told himself, standing to his feet for a better view.

A green-gold orb shone in the distance.

"It's him," Mordechi whispered. "He's coming for me!"

Mordechi snatched his boots and the satchel full of money and wriggled his way through the thorns. By the time he freed himself from the tangled growth, his feet were cut and bleeding. He rolled to his back to pull his boots on. As he slipped his left foot into the second boot, the light of the lantern reflected on the back of his hands.

It was too late to run. The ghost was on him. Looking up into the darkness of his own making, Mordechi felt sharp, bony fingers closing on his neck. A final scream died in his throat.

Two days later, a man hunting for deer came across the headless body of Mordechi Luggs, curled in a ball among the vines. He also found a torn blanket in the nearby thicket, but no leather satchel full of money.

"No need to get myself involved in this mess," he mumbled as he went about his business.

Life along Mingo Creek returned to normal. Harvest was nearly complete. Carrie, David, the Pelzers, and the other nearby families readied for winter. Carrie went daily to the barn to get hay for her horses, no longer afraid of the place or its former inhabitant.

The barn served a good many purposes. It held plenty of hay to last the whole winter; it was a warm place for mama horses to give birth to their foals; and it was home to several families of field mice. Each corner of the barn was piled high with hay.

During the winter following the ghostly visit, three of the corner piles shrank considerably. But not the pile in the corner closest to the creek — it always stayed full.

One evening after supper, Carrie and David sat at the kitchen table. "Must be that old ghost was released from its earthly bond and don't need to come around no more," Carrie said.

"Yep, I reckon so. I just wish I knew where that rotten snake Mordechi ended up. And what he did with all our money. I don't even know how much there was."

"Oh, I'm guessing Mordechi Luggs got his just deserts in the end and I'll bet that money ends up someplace useful."

"Well, guess we'll never know," sighed David.

"Yep, I guess we'll never know," Carrie echoed, turning away to hide the sly grin that curled her lips.

As far as David or Mr. Pelzer knew, Mordechi escaped with the money. No one ever found out the truth. But whenever somebody in those parts fell on hard times, good things appeared on their doorstep: food, clothing, maybe even a new horse – whatever was needed to get folks going again.

Not a single soul ever discovered who was behind all the good deeds. Some folks started whispering amongst themselves, "Maybe it's the ghost of Mingo Creek."

In the south-central region of Oklahoma lies the city of Ardmore. Once a vibrant oil town, the city has fluctuated between times of prosperity and misfortune. Currently, the city boasts a population of nearly 25,000 residents. Perfectly situated between Dallas and Oklahoma City, Ardmore maintains its status as the hub of Arbuckle country, with several lakes and other popular outdoor attractions nearby. The streets and people still reflect a simpler time and a strong sense of Oklahoma culture. When asked if there are any ghosts in Ardmore, long-time residents simply nod. "Oh, yeah, we know about ghosts."

Old Man Apple among the living

In 1978, Rhonda Fletcher and her big brother Gary lived just south of the giant water tower that watched over downtown Ardmore like some colossal B-movie robot. While the teenagers were more interested in disco dancing and muscle cars, the younger kids enjoyed simply riding their banana seat bicycles and playing in the park.

Sometimes Gary was a good big brother; sometimes he was not. He was tall and thin with straight, dishwater-blonde hair. A sixth grader, Gary played baseball and basketball and ran on the track team. Rhonda was in the fourth grade and wore her light brown hair shorter than most girls because it was so curly and tangly.

After school one day, Rhonda sat down with a peanut butter and jelly sandwich to finish her math homework. Gary burst into the room and threw his own schoolbooks on the table, sending papers flying in all directions.

"Watch it!" warned Rhonda.

"No homework today, Mom!" Gary shouted toward the back of the house. "I'm going to the park."

"Be home by dark," called their mother from the back room.

Gary sneered at his sister.

"What?" she asked. Gary snatched her sandwich and ran out the door. She started to yell for their mother, but Gary was long gone. "Bully," she cried and pulled Cocoa, her stuffed monkey and best friend, to her chest.

Rhonda soon joined her friends at the park, where the most popular play area was a long concrete basketball court surrounded by sycamores. Unspoken playground rules gave one side of the cement slab to the boys for shooting baskets, while the girls roller-skated or played hopscotch on the other.

Rhonda's second-best friend Sarah was drawing out hopscotch squares with a piece of chalk. Without warning, a basketball bounced to the girls' side and hit Sarah in the nose.

"Oops," said Bradley Hinton, one of Gary's friends. "Maybe you girls should go play somewhere else."

"Why don't you boys?" answered Rhonda. Her grip tightened around Cocoa's arm.

"Cause we're bigger," snarled Bradley with his thin milky lips.

"We're not scared of you."

"Ha. You're scared of everything."

"Am not."

"Sure you are," he said, "That's why you carry that stupid monkey everywhere."

Rhonda pulled Cocoa close and winced. Seeing his opening, Bradley lunged at her with the basketball, faking a hard pass to her face. Rhonda jumped back in surprise. He chuckled, causing his pointy nose to twitch. "See? I made you flinch, scaredy."

"Not because I was scared, Ratface. It's because I have enough sense to get out of the way. I'm not scared of anything you can dish out." When she heard herself say the word Ratface, Rhonda felt a twang of guilt. She had heard other girls call him that and knew it probably hurt his feelings. But it was too late to take the words back.

Gary stepped between his friend and his sister. He didn't like anyone else pestering her. That was his job. "You guys knock it off."

"Yeah! Just leave us alone."

Bradley turned away, laughing. "Rhonda is a scaredy-cat," he sang.

"I am not scared," she said, wiping a tear from her eye.

"Then prove it," Bradley said. "Go run around Mr. Apple's grave. Tonight."

A lump formed in Rhonda's throat. "I can't tonight. It's a school night."

"Then tomorrow."

Rhonda looked at Sarah, who shook her head and whispered, "Don't do it!"

Gary only shrugged and said, "Sorry, Sis. You set yourself up for this one."

"Fine," said Rhonda. "I'll show you who's the scaredy-cat. But you and Gary have to do it too."

Every kid in town knew about Mr. Apple's grave and the ghost that haunted it. The stories say that Mr. Apple had been a man who hated children so much he threw sharp rocks at any child who crossed his yard. Rhonda twisted beneath her blankets all night in a fit of tormenting dreams. Lumbering apples with gaping mouths and razor teeth chased her across the park. When the light of morning woke her, she had an upset stomach and her head hurt from the night's bothered sleep.

Her mother popped her head through the door with a smile in her voice. "Get up, sweetheart. Time for school."

"I don't feel good, Mom," Rhonda whined.

"C'mon, Sweetie. It's too early in the school year for missing any days."

Rhonda took far too long getting dressed. When she finally sat down at the breakfast table, Gary was already there. "Trying to play hookie, are ya?" he taunted. "I thought you wasn't scared?"

"I'm not scared," she sputtered through gritted teeth and Cheerios.

The rest of the day was agonizing. It seemed every girl in school stopped to tell her, "You're so brave" and "Go show the boys who's better." It only made things worse.

After the final bell, Bradley walked by and poked her arm. "Don't chicken out."

"*You* don't chicken out," was all she could think to say back.

"Then be at the park after dinner. We'll ride our bikes from there."

It was already dark when Gary, Bradley, and Rhonda approached the cemetery gate. A line of ominous, moonlit oaks guarded the entrance and seemed alive as they shivered in the light breeze. Rhonda lifted her book bag from her handlebars and draped the strap around her shoulder.

"Last chance to chicken out," Bradley said.

Saying nothing, she sucked in a deep breath and walked toward the gate. The rusted hinges squealed with protest when she pushed it open. Rhonda pulled a silver flashlight from her bag. The light was a great source of strength and comfort for Rhonda, but even more so was the stuffed monkey nestled deeper in the bag. She took Cocoa out with her other hand

and held the monkey close. As the three walked deeper into the graveyard, Bradley howled, "AH-ROOOO," toward the hidden moon.

"You aren't scaring me," said Rhonda, "and you're not funny either." The beam of light swept in front of Rhonda and chiseled grave stones sprang from the ground like scattered rows of giants' teeth.

"Which way?" she asked.

Gary pointed ahead and they followed his gaze. "Tommy Akers says it's more in the middle. And it's a tomb, not a grave."

The cemetery at night was the darkest and creepiest place Rhonda had ever seen. Up ahead, glowed the silhouette of two grave houses, outlined by the silvery yellow of the low-lying moon. The wind brushed the back of Rhonda's neck causing her to shudder. Her light shone across the first small building and the word APPLE appeared above the door.

"This m...m...must be it," said Rhonda. "What now?"

"You gotta knock on the door and say 'Mr. Apple, are you home?' Then run around it three times and his ghost will come chase you," said Gary.

The night air grew even darker as the moon rose and slid behind a bank of clouds. The sudden sound of dogs barking in the distance made Rhonda jump.

"What's the matter? You scared now?" Bradley taunted. Rhonda shook her head.

"Then go knock."

"You go knock."

"I ain't the one who's supposed to prove I ain't scared."

Rhonda stood before the looming grave house. Her teeth began to chatter. She took one step toward the door then pulled her foot back.

"I'll do it," said Gary. "But we all gotta run." Gary shuffled to the huge iron door. He looked one last time at the two behind him. Rhonda and Bradley nodded.

In one quick motion, Gary slammed his palm against the heavy door.

"Mr. Apple, are you home?"

Gary turned from the door and shot through the darkness at full speed. He circled the grave house three times, then veered to the path with his sister and Bradley tight on his heels. When he felt safe again, he stopped and put his hands on his knees to catch his breath while the others caught up.

"I don't see anything," he panted. They all turned toward Mr. Apple's grave and Rhonda aimed her light.

"Me neither," said Bradley. "See. Nothing to be scared of, Rhonda."

Then Rhonda's flashlight blinked and went dark.

"Turn it back on!" squealed Bradley.

"I didn't turn it off," said Rhonda. No one moved. Rhonda felt her hair standing up. The air grew heavy and the sound of crackling electricity surrounded them.

"What's that?" Bradley whimpered.

From Mr. Apple's grave a thin streak of blue-white light spread along the ground. They watched in horror as the slow-moving bolt curled in on itself and formed a ball.

"Run!" Gary commanded, as the lightning globe shot in their direction.

"He's after us!" shouted Bradley, turning on his heels.

The three regretful ghost hunters ran with all their might as the sound of sizzling air came closer. The two boys passed her and Rhonda felt heat on the back of her neck.

Up ahead she saw Gary slowing down. Bradley ran past him as her brother spun around. "Hurry, Rhonda. Keep running," Gary shouted.

She sped by her brother as he faced the lightning ball with his arms lifted and his hands spread in front of him. Rhonda heard her brother shriek. She slowed enough to twist her head around without falling. The crackling ball of light was attacking Gary. Rhonda stopped.

"Keep running!" Gary shouted between yelps of pain.

But Rhonda stood her ground. She reached into her bag and pulled out Cocoa.

Gary ran to her side and grabbed her by the arm. "C'mon, run!"

Rhonda held the stuffed monkey by the legs and swung at the ball of light. The sizzling globe danced around their heads. Cocoa acted as a shield, as they half ran and half twisted toward the cemetery gate.

"There's the gate," cried Gary, pulling Rhonda along.

Rhonda tucked a now smoldering Cocoa beneath her arm and ran full-out. With just ten yards to go, their feet became tangled and Gary tumbled forward, dragging Rhonda down with him. They jumped to their feet and turned back to look. The ball was coming straight for their faces. Rhonda hurled Cocoa toward the light.

POP! POP! ...POP!

The orb exploded, sending sparks and electric tentacles high into the night sky. When the embers settled, nothing remained but darkness and the sound of barking dogs in the distance.

Rhonda and Gary slowly stood and steadied themselves on each other, then wobbled to their bikes.

"Where's Bradley?" Rhonda asked, noting his missing bike.

"Probably under his bed by now," Gary answered. They both laughed. "I never thought I'd be so glad to see Cocoa!"

When Gary and Rhonda walked through the front door, Mom and Dad were sitting on the sofa. "You guys are home kinda late," Dad started.

"Sorry, Dad," they said together. Without thinking, Gary lifted his hand and rubbed the burning welts that dotted the back of his neck.

"What's wrong with your neck, Gary?" asked Mom, standing to her feet and taking a closer look. He stammered, not sure what to say, but his mother never gave him a chance.

"I know those welts," she said. "Mr. Apple's grave. Are you kidding me?" She turned toward their dad. "Do you see what your children have been doing," she said frantically and dashed into the kitchen.

"It's all right, honey. They're home safe, now," said their father. As he followed their Mom, Rhonda and Gary noticed that he was rubbing his own neck. They turned toward each other with the realization that their parents were remembering a long-ago scary night of their own.

3
Jimmie the Doodlebug

When large pools of oil were discovered beneath the ground in Oklahoma, the state went crazy with Black Gold Fever. Poor people got rich and rich people got richer as oilmen from around the world appeared, anxious to dig in Oklahoma soil. The hard part was deciding where to drill. An oil company could spend thousands of dollars to drill a well that came up dry. Only a few hundred yards away, another company's well could strike it rich.

Many companies employed geologists to study land formations and locate the best places to drill. Less practical oil seekers employed men who claimed to have a spiritual connection to the ground, a connection that "told" them where to drill. These men were called "doodlebugs" and they had unique ways of finding oil. Some said they could just smell the oil, others used strange machines made of pressure gauges and copper tubing, and still others used some form of divining rod, a forked stick that shivered when held over an oil deposit. Most of the doodlebugs proved to be fakes, but a few of the best have been remembered as "the real deal" because of their impressive string of good finds. One well-respected oilman said that back in the early days of the Oklahoma oil business, one doodlebug story stood above the rest -- the story of Jimmie Hudgins.

In 1934, Jimmie Hudgins was ten years old. Jimmie's family, like most Oklahoma folks of the Great Depression era, was dirt poor. Their wood frame house lay in a valley among the rolling hills of northeast Oklahoma. On Sunday nights the church choir practiced, and the small valley filled with the sound of old hymns floating on the breeze.

One night while walking home from church with his mother, Jimmie asked, "When you bring those jars of food with you, it's for the really poor folks that can't grow their own, right Mama?"

"That's right, dear," his mother replied. "We ought to give whenever we can."

"Well, when I get big, I'm gonna give to the hungry folks."

"That's good, Jimmie. That'll make Jesus real happy."

The next week, Jimmie again went to choir practice with his mother.

"I'll wait for you outside," he told his mother, opening the church door for her.

"Okay, dear. Just don't go too far."

As the night sky darkened, Jimmie made his way to a tire swing hung from the gnarled branch of a giant tree behind the church. Jimmie sat in the swing and twisted around and around, then lifted his feet and spun the other direction. Slowly at first, then twirling faster and faster, Jimmie leaned his head back and looked toward the sky. The stars became a blur, streaking like comets racing in circles. The swing slowed and he put his feet on the worn dirt. *This is even more fun than putting frogs down the back of Nancy Culligan's dress*, he thought.

Jimmie closed his eyes to make the spinning in his head stop. When he opened them again, he felt something was wrong.

Things were too quiet. He no longer heard the choir singing from the church.

The surrounding forest, usually alive with the noise of crickets, hoot owls, and tree frogs, was soundless. Jimmie thought he had gone deaf. He snapped his fingers next to each ear to make sure they still worked. From the darkness up the hill he heard a voice calling his name.

"Jim…mie," it rasped.

"Jim…mie Hud…gins." It came from the old cemetery.

"Who is it?" Jimmie hollered, walking toward the voice.

"It's Uncle Felix."

"B...but…you're s'posed to be dead. We buried you three years ago."

"Oh, I'm dead alright, Jimmie," the spirit voice answered. "Come closer. I have something to tell you."

"I can hear ya just fine. Tell me from there. I don't wanna come any closer."

The ghost of Uncle Felix began to sing:

> *The oil in the ground, it sings a song,*
> *And I can hear it all night long.*
> *If you're good and do no wrong,*
> *I'll share with you the oil's song.*

"What's that mean?" asked Jimmie.

"It means you and your family can be rich, boy. I can tell you where there's oil in the ground and then you can tell them oilmen where to dig their wells. They'll give you lots of money for doin' this."

"You can do that?"

"I sure can, Jimmie-Boy. But if I do, you must always use the money for good. Care for your family and help the poor. You must never be selfish or bad. And most important of all…are you listening, boy?"

"Yes, Uncle Felix."

"Most important of all, you must never tell anyone about me."

"How am I s'posed to find the oilmen and how am I gonna get them to listen to me? Uncle Felix, I'm just a boy."

"But you're a smart boy, and you'll figure it out."

Jimmie heard his mother's voice calling from the front of the church.

"Be good, Jimmie," Uncle Felix whispered.

"Wait. Uncle Felix?"

"Be good…"

The voice was gone. The rhythmic song of crickets and other night sounds returned. Jimmie felt as if he had just come back to the living world. He raced down the hill and around the church to join his mother.

On the walk home, Jimmie was silent. How am I going to get my folks to let me go find the oilmen? And if I do find some oilmen, how will I get them to dig a well where I say? These questions and more wrestled in Jimmie's mind.

Then it struck him. Jimmie remembered that his big sister Katie and her new husband John lived in Glenpool, where lots of oilmen were. Katie was a school teacher, and since it was a well-known fact that Jimmie wasn't so interested in schoolwork, he came up with the perfect plan.

"Mama? Can I go stay with Katie for awhile? I think she could help me with my reading and stuff. It's probably time I learn a few things that might be important when I grow up."

His mother was so happy, she talked to his father that night and they agreed that a few months in Glenpool might do Jimmie some good. Later that night, the words *And do no wrong* came back to haunt Jimmie.

"Did I just tell my mama a lie?" he asked himself. "No," he decided, "not if I make myself want to learn to read better and all that school stuff." Once he convinced himself that he really did want to learn, Jimmie realized he had told his mama the truth all along.

Two days later his father took him to the train station. "I wired Katie and told her you wanted to come stay awhile. She'll be waitin' for you when you get there. So stay out of trouble, son. And do everythin' she tells you. And Jimmie, I'm real proud of you for wantin' to learn."

"Thanks, Poppa. And don't worry none. I'll be good."

Katie's warm hugs and big smile greeted Jimmie at the train depot. They walked home through the busy streets of Glenpool. Jimmie searched the many faces for an oilman, realizing he wouldn't know it if he saw one.

"Katie, do you know any oilmen?"

"John drives a truck for the oilfields. So yeah, I know some oilmen."

"Do you think I could meet one some time?"

"Sure, Jimmie. You can meet an oilman. I'll bet on days you aren't in school you could maybe even go with John in his truck."

The smile on Jimmie's face widened to a big fat-cat grin.

"But only as long as your reading improves," his sister added.

The next few weeks, Jimmie settled in to his new daily routine. He went to school everyday with Katie. He even began to like reading and learning. He brought home books everyday and started reading just for fun. He was also getting used to his new home. John worked long hours and often spent nights away from home carrying pipes and other materials out to the oil wells.

"John?" asked Jimmie one night at dinner. "Can I go to work with you sometime? I've been doin' real good at school and all. Please?"

John looked at his wife. Katie shrugged her shoulders and smiled.

"I don't see why not. I could sure use the company. It gets awful boring sometimes driving all that way by myself. But it has to be when you don't have school."

"Tomorrow's no school," blurted Jimmie.

John chuckled. "Oh, really. Well, I guess it's tomorrow then."

Early the next morning, John and Jimmie climbed into the truck.

"Don't forget these!" Katie handed John two small sacks through the driver's side window. Each sack held a ham sandwich and carrots. "Be careful and I'll see you tonight."

The roads to the oil wells were rough and muddy. The truck's engine ground forward, coughing black smoke as it crawled along. Jimmie met several of the men John worked with, but none of them were the men who decided where to drill for oil. After darkness settled, John turned the truck toward home. The truck's headlights cast dancing shadows along the sides of the long and twisting dirt road.

As they passed a wide open field, Jimmie heard a humming sound in his ears. "Stop the truck!" he shouted.

"What is it, Jimmie?"

"I think I hear singing from out in that field." The door flew open as Jimmie leaped to the ground.

"Jimmie!" John hollered. "Wait up! Whatcha runnin' for?" But Jimmie was already half-way to the middle of the field before John could catch up. The grass hid Jimmie's waist as he glided away from the truck.

The song grew louder in Jimmie's head. "Can you hear that? The music. And the singing."

"I don't hear nothing."

Only Jimmie could hear as the words to the song took shape.

> *The oil in the ground, it sings a song,*
> *And I can hear it all night long.*
> *If you're good and do no wrong,*
> *I'll share with you the oil's song.*

"It's here," Jimmie shouted. "Right here."

"What's here?"

"Oil. It's right here in the ground beneath us -- and lots of it."

"Jimmie, you're actin' crazy. Now quit it. Get in the truck. We're goin' home."

"John. You gotta believe me. I know for a fact there's oil right here. You gotta tell your boss to drill right here in this field."

"Oh, so you're some kinda doodlebug, are ya? That you can just find oil without knowing anything about drilling or geology? And what makes you so sure of this oil being here?"

"I dunno," said Jimmie. "I can just feel it is all. And hear it. There starts a humming in my ear when I get close to the oil and it turns to a kinda song when I get to the right spot."

"That's the durndest thing I ever heard, Jimmie." John chuckled as he climbed into the cab of his truck.

The two were silent most of the way home. John kept looking at Jimmie as if he were waiting for the joke to become obvious…for Jimmie to start laughing…or at least to crack a smile. But he never did.

As they pulled into town, Jimmie turned toward John.

"It's true, John. There's oil back there and if we can get someone to drill right where I said, we're all gonna be rich."

The next day, John went to his boss, E.B. O'Brien, the wealthiest oilman around.

"I know it's weird, Mr. O'Brien, but I believe him. It was the strangest thing ever, that look on his face, almost like he really was hearing music."

"Well, I've certainly heard of stranger ways of findin' oil. I'll send some of my guys to that field and check it out." O'Brien sent both geologists and drillers. They put in a well and when they had drilled twelve hundred feet below ground, they struck a large deposit of oil. Mr. O'Brien, amazed and grateful for their help, gave John and Jimmie four hundred dollars. When the well continued to pump oil, he laid ten more crisp one hundred dollar bills in Jimmie's hand. "Any more hunches on where to drill?" he asked.

Once again, John and Jimmie climbed in the rickety old truck and drove all day. Jimmie sat on the lumpy seat, waiting for his ears to hum. "I think maybe it only works at night," he sighed.

"Then night it will be," John answered. For two weeks they crisscrossed backcountry roads. Finally, Jimmie heard it again.

> *The oil in the ground, it sings a song,*
> *And I can hear it all night long.*
> *If you're good and do no wrong,*
> *I'll share with you the oil's song.*

The next day, John told Mr. O'Brien of their discovery. The oilman shuffled his feet back and forth as if he were trying to dance, then hollered "Yippee" at the top of his lungs.

"You keep this up, son, and you're gonna be the richest boy in the whole world." That sounded pretty good to Jimmie, but he remembered Uncle Felix's warning.

For the next two years, John and Jimmie traveled throughout Oklahoma for Mr. O'Brien and he gave them piles of money. True to his word, Jimmie shared with the poor. He gave to soup kitchens, hospitals, charities, and never told a soul about Uncle Felix's ghost.

With all the to-and-fro of oil hunting, Jimmie quit reading. He missed the fun of it, but he didn't have the time. He became a respected young man in the oil towns and gradually grew tired, even ashamed, of his worn clothing.

He bought a new suit. *Just once, something for me.* Then he needed some shiny new boots to match his three new suits. And a gold ring to let people know he was a man to be taken seriously. Though the old truck ran fine, Jimmie felt he and John should ride in style; he bought them a new truck. He still gave money to charity, but not nearly as much. It never dawned on Jimmie that Uncle Felix's song was appearing less and less often.

One night when Jimmie was fourteen, he rode with John down a long and rugged dirt road. In dark comfort, the click-click of the engine played a soft lullaby. The rocking back and forth of the cab made Jimmie's eyes grow heavy. He leaned his head against the window and nodded off to sleep.

"Jimmie, wake up!" John nudged Jimmie on the shoulder. "Do you hear any singing yet?"

"No," said Jimmie, rubbing his eyes. "Uncle Felix ain't sung in awhile now." Immediately Jimmie realized his mistake.

"What does your Uncle Felix have to do with it?"

"Nothing."

John kept asking and Jimmie denied saying anything about Uncle Felix. But it was too late. He had already said it. "I have to go home…not your home…my folks' home…my home."

Jimmie's parents smothered him in their arms. He had missed them greatly and was glad to be home. His mother made a special meal.

At supper he told them of all the exciting things he had seen at the oilfields, of all the towns they had been to around the state, places like Tulsa, Seminole, and Elk City. He told them of all the strange people he had seen, like the cowboys and Indians of the Wild West shows and the rodeos. But no matter how joyful he seemed, there was a feeling of great loss in his chest. Finished eating, he scooted away from the table and stood. "I'll be back after while. I'm goin' for a walk."

"All right, dear. But don't go too far," his mother told him.

He walked to the church in darkness. Beneath his arm he carried a bundle wrapped in parchment paper. He put the package holding all of his suits on the doorway of the church, before walking up the hill, past the tire swing, and to the graveyard. In the moonlight, he found Uncle Felix's gravestone and knelt.

"I'm sorry, Uncle Felix. I didn't mean to. It was an accident."

There was no answer.

"Uncle Felix. Talk to me, I'm sorry."

The surrounding trees were deathly quiet; no chatter from the nighttime forest creatures interrupted Jimmie's plea for his uncle's return. Jimmie saw a thick fog spreading across the ground, as the smoky outline of a man appeared.

"Jim…mie," rasped his Uncle's voice. "Follow me."

Jimmie followed the specter up the hill deeper into the fog and toward the sharp cliffs on the other side.

Jimmie was never seen in the oilfields again. Many of the oilmen told stories of how a ghost led Jimmie over a cliff to his death, and how a bundle of his fancy suits had mysteriously appeared on the doorsteps of the local church.

But that was just legend. Jimmie stayed in the comfortable home with his parents, reading all the great books of the world, until he went away to college. He once told his mother about the ghost of her brother Felix and recalled those final words on the foggy hilltop.

"Can I please have my gift back?" he had pleaded with his uncle.

"Jim-mie," the ghost whispered. "The gift was never the song. You never lost the real gift I gave. It will serve you well."

"What is the gift, then?" Jimmie asked.

"You will know." The apparition faded back into the fog. "Be good…"

Those were the last words he ever heard from Uncle Felix's ghost, and never again did the song ring in his ears.

When Jimmie got older, his passion for the written word led him to become a teacher and a writer. He always remembered the promise he had made that night walking home with his Mother – that he would give greatly to the poor and starving. But Jimmy gave more than food: he fed people hungry for words of encouragement and imagination. He lifted young minds away from thoughts of greed and toward lives of giving. He discovered that this was the real treasure Uncle Felix spoke of, the gifts of inspiration and compassion.

A lifetime later, when Jimmie had died an old man, he was buried in that cemetery behind the church in the valley. Many former students, who had also become writers and teachers, came to the funeral services. A few who lingered by the graveside as the sun set and darkness settled, heard a distant singing. And in the voice of Jimmie Hudgins, the greatest doodlebug of all, they heard this song, floating on the wind.

> *Words on a page are better than gold,*
> *And you will find as your lives unfold,*
> *That money is nothing to the final host,*
> *For the truly good, have given the most.*

"Be good…" the voice whispered, and then there was silence.

The Boy Who Cried Lion

On a single April day in 1889, Oklahoma City was born. Ten thousand homesteaders created a city of white canvas tents that stretched for miles along the North Canadian River. Starting in the 1920's, thousands upon thousands of rural folks moved to "The City" looking for work in the larger factories. This flood of new people soon created the state's largest metropolitan area. Surrounding the city's suburban neighborhoods were vast expanses of undeveloped grasslands and wooded areas. A young boy's imagination could run wild in this edge-of-the-city wilderness. But it wasn't just the imagination running wild. Sometimes it was a fierce beast, lurking in the dark, waiting to pounce.

Lee Roberts won this new bicycle from the newspaper

Local Boy Captures Lion

Mrs. Ernestine Lancaster became a librarian to make a difference in the lives of children. After 18 years, she still felt that connecting just the right book with just the right child was the most precious gift she could give--even if she rarely got any thanks for it. *Just once*, she often thought, *I'd like to know I truly made a difference.*

On a warm fall day in 1957, nine year old Lee Roberts rushed home from school to tell his family all about the news of the day. The headline of *The Daily Oklahoman* read ESCAPED LION TERRORIZES CITY. All the school kids were talking about it and a good many grown-ups, too. Around the dinner table it was the only topic of discussion.

"Ryan Henderson says it's the biggest lion ever in captivity," said Lee.

"Becky Davenport says that lions like to eat only boys," added Lee's big sister Vera, "Because of how mean you both are. It's only natural."

"Vera, quit scaring your brother," said their father. "You have nothing to worry about, Lee. The circus grounds are more than five miles from here."

"Ryan also said lions like to live in the *sur-vanna*; you know, big places full of tall grass. Just like the fields on the other side of 99th Street."

"The word you're trying to say is *savanna* and you'll see, they'll catch this lion in no time. Every officer in the city is out there right now searching. Now, that's enough talk about lions. Eat your peas," commanded his mother.

Lee was the local paperboy. Early every morning two bundles of *The Daily Oklahoman* appeared on the Roberts' doorstep. Lee rolled and wrapped each paper with a rubber band. By 5:30 a.m., with a stuffed bag over his shoulders, he would be pedaling his bicycle and tossing papers throughout the neighborhood. Though still quite young in the eyes of the world, Lee had mastered the skillful art of any great paperboy. He held the handlebars with his left hand and tossed the papers in a high arc over his head with his right. By the time he reached the next house, he'd have another paper ready to throw. He rarely missed.

The final mile of his route was Lee's favorite time of the morning. The houses grew further apart, separated by open fields of tall grass the color of honey. As the first hint of daylight graced the morning after the lion's escape, Lee turned east on 99th street. Pedaling up the last hill, he heard a fierce growl coming from behind.

It's the lion, he thought. *It's gonna eat me.*

Lee threw all of his eighty-seven pounds into his flight up the hill, pedaling for his life. He heard a loud bark and was relieved to see Sparky, the Ledbetters' German shepherd. Sparky chased him often, but never attacked. "Go away, Sparky," Lee shouted. "Go home."

Lee slowed his bike, grabbed a paper, and readied himself for 99th Street. He flung a paper onto Mr. Beasley's porch and coasted down the hill. His mind at ease, Lee gazed across the field. In the dark morning shadows he saw two orange-yellow glowing dots coming from the edge of the trees. He stopped his bike and stared.

What is that? The spots didn't move. Then one flickered. *Like a blink. Wait! They really are eyes, and they're looking straight at me!* He shielded his vision against the first rays of the sun and squinted. The outline of a face took shape. Then a pointy ear twitched and he made out a hairy mane. It was the lion. This time, he was sure.

The color of the huge cat blended perfectly with the grass. The lion was nearly invisible except for those glowing eyes. Fear clutched his mind, as Lee pedaled furiously for home.

Reaching his yard, he dropped the bicycle and ran inside. In one swift motion he flung open the door, slammed it, and locked it. Lee stood against the door panting for breath.

"What in the world are you doing?" asked his mother.

"Lion…behind me," was all he was able to say.

She lifted the curtains and looked out front, then turned to face him with her hands on her hips.

"First of all, Lee Allen Roberts, I don't see any lion. Second, why are we locking the door? Lions cannot open doors. Now stop this foolishness. Is your route finished?" Lee's lowered chin and slumped shoulders gave Mrs. Roberts her answer. "People are expecting their morning papers, Lee."

"I know, Mom. But there's a lion loose on 99th Street. I saw it. It had orange glowing eyes and a big mane. And it looked hungry."

"Oh, son, you have such an imagination. I'll drive you to school. We can finish your route on the way. After school you are going to apologize to everyone for being late with the paper. And if I hear one more mention of lions, you'll never watch television again."

Lee tried telling his friends at school that he had seen the lion. But no one believed him, not even his best friend Glen, who had suggested that he was probably going crazy and just seeing things.

Angry at everyone, Lee avoided people as best he could for the rest of the day. After school, he retraced his route and apologized to his morning customers.

That night at the supper table, his two younger brothers roared under their breaths and giggled. "Not at the table, boys," chided their mother.

"Everyone at school was talking about how Lee thinks he's some kind of famous lion hunter," added Vera.

Lee spent the evening in his room with the door shut. *At least tomorrow is Saturday. I won't have to listen to no one laughing at me...if I catch the lion...that would prove I'm not a liar.*

Lee spent the rest of the evening plotting, planning, and scribbling ideas in his notebook. As he drifted off to sleep around eleven, one question remained, *How am I going to catch that lion?*

Even though the Saturday edition was thicker, Lee raced through the neighborhood and tossed papers faster than normal. He kept a watchful eye on the field as he pedaled up 99th Street but saw nothing. When the last paper left his hand, he sped home to start his lion hunt. *If only I had a tranquilizer gun*, he thought.

Lee looked in the garage for anything that would work. *A net would work. Or a deep pit, maybe.* But he didn't have a net and he had tried to dig deep holes before. The red Oklahoma clay was much too hard. *The library. They'll have a book on how catch big animals.*

Lee pedaled furiously to the library. He had always been a little afraid of Mrs. Lancaster, but this time he approached her bravely. "Do you have any books on catching lions?"

"Oh, I am sure we do," she said with a warm and proud smile. "Look on the shelf in the section numbered 799.29, Big Game Hunting." Lee was soon flipping through the pages of the perfect book for trapping animals.

"Thank you so much, Mrs. Lancaster. I think you just saved a bunch of people," he said, running for the door. He never saw the puzzled look on her face as she asked herself, *what in the world is that boy up to now?* But she did smile at the thought that at least someone considered her a hero.

Lee thumbed through pages of drawings of traps and snares until he found what he was looking for – a simple trap he just might be able to build himself.

The trap consisted of three basic parts – two ropes, bait, and a counterweight – and he had them all. His father had plenty of rope in the garage. *Okay, so I don't have a counter weight. But how hard can that be to make? I can pile my sister's sleeping bag full of rocks for a counter weight. Okay, but what to use as bait?* That answer was easy – roast beef!

Every Sunday, Lee's mother prepared a big after-church dinner, the one meal all week long no one was allowed to miss. He would be in the biggest trouble of his life when his mom went to the freezer and found the roast missing. *But it's worth it, it has to be done.*

By late afternoon, Lee found enough rocks to fill the sleeping bag, tied the ropes on each end, and heaved the bag on to a thick tree branch eight feet off the ground. The ropes dangled on either side of the limb.

Lee pulled one rope to a hiding place in the nearby bushes and tied a loop at the end of the other rope. He half-buried the roast inside the loop.

The plan was for the lion to come for the roast. Since it was partially buried, the lion couldn't immediately grab the meat and run. He would have to dig with his front paws. As soon as his paws were inside the loop, Lee would tug on the longer rope, sending the sleeping bag falling to the ground, thereby lifting the helpless lion up by the legs. Lee would then dash for help

When the trap was set, Lee lay in his hiding place between two fallen tree trunks covered with bushes. He could barely see the tree, but he was close enough to hear when the lion came. So the waiting began.

Lying in the darkness, Lee realized maybe this was not such a good idea. *Maybe the rope's not strong enough; maybe there aren't enough rocks in the bag. Even worse, what if the lion has set a trap for me and I'm laying in it? It could be watching me right now, creeping closer.* Chills ran up his spine. Lee shifted so he could look around for the glowing orange. Through the trees, he caught the slight shifting shadows of movement in the dark. He heard a grunting-growl and the sound of digging coming from the trap area. He jerked on the rope in his hands and the sleeping bag fell. A loud, sharp yelp belted through the grove of trees.

"I got him!" Lee jumped from his hiding place and saw the silhouette of a four-legged body dangling from the rope, writhing to get free. A growling, high-pitched whine came from the beast--nothing like the sound Lee imagined a lion would make.

Lee shined the light on his catch. It was not the lion. It was Sparky, the Fletchers' German shepherd.

"Darn it, Sparky. What are you doing here?" The dog looked at Lee with big helpless eyes. "Alright, boy. Hold still. I'll get you down."

Lee loosened the loop and Sparky dropped. The dog lifted its paws to Lee's chest. He scratched Sparky behind the ears, feeling a bit relieved. Even though Sunday dinner was wasted, and he would be punished, at least he didn't have to face the lion.

"C'mon, boy. Let's get you home."

Lee turned toward the row of lighted windows on 99th Street in the distance. Walking through the tall grass, Lee stopped. A sudden lump of fear wedged deep in the pit of his stomach. Up ahead, he saw orange glowing eyes watching his every move. Those eyes stood between him and safety. Sparky saw them, too. He barked, growled, and fiercely bared his teeth.

The lion lifted from the grass and crept toward dog and boy. Sparky pranced back and forth guarding Lee. The big cat shook its mane and roared.

Lee backed into the trees. He never took his eyes from the lion's own stare. *I can't outrun it...and lions can climb trees.* Lee's mind raced frantically for an escape plan as the lion crept forward. As he reached the circle of trees where the trap was, Lee felt his ankle catch in the rope that now lay on the ground. It had fallen from the tree branch. The lion moved closer, watching both boy and dog.

Lee gathered the looped end of the rope and readied for the lion. It was a desperate plan. He would only get one chance. Lee lifted the loop above his head. The lion entered the circle of trees and shifted back on its hind legs, ready to pounce. As fully-extended claws sliced through the air, Lee let loose. The rope spiraled and circled the lion's neck.

"Run, Sparky!" Lee shouted, as he turned and dashed away. The lion roared even louder and chased after him, dragging the sleeping bag full of rocks. The added weight had little effect on the lion. The ferocious beast was gaining.

Lee ran faster than he ever had in his life. Leaping between two trunks of a Y-shaped tree, he rolled to his knees. But the landing was hard and he twisted his ankle. Pain shot up his left leg. He fell back to the ground as Sparky landed next to him. Trying again to stand, Lee realized it was useless. He couldn't run fast enough with a hurt ankle. Sparky regained his defiant stance as the lion leaped through the Y of the tree. At the same moment, Lee reached to the ground for a fallen branch he could use as a club.

Sparky charged the lion with a fierce attack toward the cat's throat. The lion swatted, sending Sparky flying through the air. He howled in pain. The orange eyes turned toward Lee. Taking a step backwards, he lifted his club. The lion kept coming. Lee swung with all his might.

But the lion gracefully shifted its head out of reach, and then leaped forward. Lee was off balance from the swing. Falling backwards, he closed his eyes, expecting the full weight of the lion and its sharp teeth to be on him before he even hit the ground.

But it didn't. Instead, Lee landed hard enough to knock the breath from his lungs. When he re-opened his eyes, he saw the fiery orange eyes a few feet from his own. The lion was pulling against the rope that held him back. The sleeping bag had lodged between the forked tree trunks and held fast. Lee scooted as best he could in a wide circle around the tree. The lion followed, twisting itself more and more in the rope.

"We did it, Sparky. We captured the lion," Lee yelled at the top of his lungs. "Let them say I made it up this time!"

By the next day, all was forgiven. Everyone in his family apologized to Lee a half-dozen times for not believing him. The Sunday dinner was filled with laughter and family joy. Lee was a hero and it didn't matter to anyone that in the center of the table sat a platter full of peanut butter and jelly sandwiches.

The next morning, Lee sat in the glow of the porch light and read the headline, LOCAL BOY CAPTURES LION. Below the large print was a big picture of his smiling face and a German shepherd licking his cheek.

Mrs. Ernestine Lancaster, the librarian, pinned a newspaper clipping to the entryway bulletin board. A wide smile lit her face. In the picture from the front page, Lee Roberts, with his arm around Sparky, smiled back. *Finally*, she thought, *I have made a difference.*

Deadman's Treasure

The mountains of southwestern Oklahoma are the dry and barren home of rattlesnakes and scorpions. But every spring the winds sweep down from the Rocky Mountains with much-needed rain. Cedars, maples, and mesquite trees drink thirstily, and soon their leaves turn green and beautiful. Overnight, the Wichita Mountains turn from a land of the dead to a treasure of colors.

Oklahoma Territory, 1905

Webster Gibbs had been walking for the last three days with little to eat and less to drink. His horse had left him four nights past when a thunderstorm cast its fury on his small camp halfway between Fort Reno and Fort Sill. Webb gave chase, but the horse's fear drove him beyond madness and the blanketing downpour soon erased his tracks.

Tired and lazy, Webster had not unsaddled the horse for the night. His error also cost him his rifle and the fifty dollars hidden in his saddlebag. All he had now was a blanket roll and his six-shooter – and even that only had five bullets.

His old boots wore thin at the soles and blisters covered his feet. The long days of dry heat had sapped most of his strength and he was about to topple over when he spied a giant oak tree spreading her shaded arms in welcome. He hurried toward the tree, but then a glorious sound stopped him in his tracks. Water! Old Webb heard the gurgling of live spring water. Racing to the nearby stream, he yanked off his boots, dropped his gunbelt, and jumped in the water fully-clothed.

Webb touched the shallow bottom, then lifted his head and shook droplets of water in all directions. He gulped in a big breath and sank once more. When his skin felt alive again, he stood in the waste-deep stream and hollered to the sky.

"I'm gonna live! You hear that, Vernon! I'm gonna make it and I'm comin' for it. The treasure's gonna be mine you thievin' scallywag."

He waded to the bank and lay in the grass and in moments was sound asleep. When he awoke he was flat on his back not far from the sheltering oak. The light was fading and Webster felt content. "I am still alive and the treasure will be mine," he said with a smile.

The sound of a snapping twig jolted Webster from his bliss. He scrambled for his gunbelt as a man stepped from behind the tree.

"I'd stop right there, if I was you," the stranger said. He was a man of not more than twenty-five, red-whiskered and holding two pistols aimed at Webster. "Where you headed?"

"Down around the Wichita Mountains."

"Is that where that treasure you was yappin' about is?"

"It's nothing," Webb said, squirming. "Just something my brother took from our home a long time ago and I come to get it back."

"What's it worth?"

"Everything," he said, grinning. The young man took a small knife and cut the strings of a leather satchel hanging from Webster's belt. He shook the bag but nothing jingled, then a folded piece of paper fell from the opening.

"What's this?"

"Just a letter."

"Well let's just read it, shall we?"

"No!" screamed Webster. "It's private."

"Is it about the treasure, old man? Let's just see."

Dearest Webb,

The local doc here says I'm soon for the Promised Land. I'm leaving you this rotten, dried-up patch of weeds I been homesteadin' for the past eight years -- if'n you want it. I reckon you'll be comin' soon enough to claim your prize and I know you'll be lookin' fer that shiny treasure that dad give me and that you been yearnin' for so long. But I git the last laugh here, cause I'm takin' it to the grave with me. And don't go thinkin' on diggin' me up, cause I found a safe hole to drop myself in where you can't find it. But I know you're gonna try. So, in parting, I'll just say watch out for the snakes.

Your brother 'cause I never had a choice –
Vernon H. Gibbs

"Well, roasted pickles, Webb! It sounds like your brother don't like you much."

"No, I s'pose he don't. Or didn't."

"And it also sounds like you under-spoke on that treasure. Sounds pretty fine to me. Maybe I'll go have a look-see."

"Please, gimme back my letter."

"What'ya think he means about snakes?"

"I dunno. He knows I hate snakes and I guess he just wants ta' rattle me some."

"Well, Mr. Webb, sir. I think I'm gonna go find out."

Webb stood on wobbly legs and started for the stranger. "Gimme that letter," he said through gritted teeth.

In one swift motion, the man lifted his gun and clubbed Webb across the temple.

It took red-bearded Farley Jenkins two and half weeks to find the location of Vernon Gibbs' homestead. Following the advice of a shopkeeper in Lawton, Farley came to a house nestled in the crooks and crannies of the Wichita Mountains. A small wagon path lead to a shack tacked together with half-rotten boards and a tin roof. He climbed from his horse and stepped toward the house when he first heard that chilling sound.

CH-CH-CH-CH-CH

Rattlesnake.

Farley reached for his pistol. The huge snake lay curled on the trail, three feet in front of him, weaving its head back and forth. He shot all six bullets at the snake. When it moved no more, he flung the carcass into a clump of mesquite trees and entered the house.

Farley ducked his head to step through the doorway and looked around the dark interior. The floor was dirt, the walls had no windows, and bundles of sage grass and small animal bones hung from leather strips tied to the rafters. A rusty bed frame and tattered mattress sat in one corner and against the back wall stood a wooden locker, a chair, and a chest of drawers with a porcelain washbin on top.

Farley looked through the locker and chest. He looked under the bed. Nothing of interest caught his eye. Walking around back, he found a well house and a barn. He pulled a bucket from the well and took a long drink. Wiping his mouth with his shirtsleeve, he walked to the barn. It was empty, except for a few tools and a rusty plow.

"It don't look like a man with any kind of treasure lived here," he said out loud.

Behind the barn, he saw a trail winding downward along the edge of a deep gully wash. Farley drew his two pistols. *If ever there was a place for snakes to live, this was it.* He saw a small, cave-like opening between two slabs of fallen rock. He edged closer and peered into the hole. *It's certainly deep enough to hide a treasure.*

Farley holstered his guns and cut a branch from a nearby scrub brush. He stuck the branch into the hole and shook it around. He hoped to scare away any snakes that might be in there, or at least get them to announce their presence with a rattle.

When he saw and heard nothing, he dropped to his knees and peered inside. It was too dark to see anything, so he crawled into the hole. He inched his way forward, feeling the walls on either side. After several feet, he felt the cave grow wider.

A slight ray of sunlight shone through a crack in the rocks above, and Farley saw before him the decaying corpse of the homesteader Vernon Gibbs. The dead man's arms were folded across his chest. He lay on the ground, covered in dust and dressed in what was most likely his best and only suit. The black cloth of the pants and coat matched the black butterfly tie around his neck.

Farley searched around the cave for piles of treasure and gold. He reckoned it must be gold because the letter said the treasure was shiny. But he saw nothing in the darkness. *Maybe he left a map*, Farley thought, searching the ground around the body. Then his eye caught the glint of shiny metal, clutched in the man's bony hands. Prying the skeletal fingers apart, he lifted a gold pocket watch on a chain. Farley bit down on the watch and ran his fingers across the surface. No tooth marks. The watch was gold-plated and practically worthless. The inscription read:

For my son, the greatest treasure a father could have.

"Okay, so where is this treasure then, old man?" Farley asked out loud.

CH-CH-CH-CH-CH-CH

The writhing serpent had slipped up behind him. Farley turned to shoot. He heard another *CH-CH-CH-CH*, then another and another. He was surrounded, yet still more rattlers added their warning of impending doom. On hands and knees, Farley scurried along the ground, but his gun belt caught on the rocks. He felt the weight of an enormous rattlesnake crawling across the back of his leg. He kicked furiously. Immediately, he felt the dagger-sharp pain shooting through his body. He reached toward the light ahead, his knees gave way, and he fell with his face in the dirt. The last thing Farley Jenkins saw was the glint of sunlight off the gold-plated watch he held in his outstretched hand.

Webster Gibbs was glad to be on his horse again. It seemed a miracle when his horse reappeared at the creek near the giant oak two days after Webb had been clubbed and left for dead. Now, three weeks later, he was nearing his brother's homestead. He had come a long way to get the treasure that should have been rightly his so long ago.

The brothers were once close, even as young men, until their father died less than a week before Christmas. On that ill-fated day, their mother brought in two boxes – each wrapped in colorful paper – but neither had a name on it.

The boys opened the two boxes. One held a shotgun and a note that simply read, *Don't shoot yourself. Love, Pa*. In the other was the watch which bore the inscription that both felt must certainly be for them.

"I'm Pa's treasure," shouted Vernon.

"NO! I am!" said Webb.

Not even their mother truly knew her husband's intent. As long as she was alive, she made the boys take turns owning the watch, changing every year. The resentment between the two brothers grew year after year, till one day Vernon disappeared with the watch.

Now he was dead and it was Webb's watch, if he could find it. With some luck and the kindness of strangers, he found his brother's rotting shack. Soon, he was treading cautiously down the rough, rocky trail behind the barn. Reaching the path's end, he saw sparkling metal. The watch!

CH-CH-CH-CH-CH

Thirty snakes, maybe more, rose from beneath the rocks. Soon they were all around him, coiled and ready to strike. Webb felt dizzy and nearly fainted. His brother would have one final laugh. Lying frozen in the sweltering heat, Webb slowly reached for the watch. If he was going to die, at least he would get to hold it one more time.

He clutched the watch and wrapped his hand around it. Every muscle tensed for the pain he knew was coming. The fattest rattler he had ever seen slithered within four inches of his face. Webb lay on the ground eyeball to eyeball with death itself. The snake flicked its forked tongue and pulled its head back to strike. Webb felt the ground shake beneath him. Something strange was happening. The watch glowed and grew warm. Though he didn't understand it, Webb felt his brother's presence and knew Vernon had spared him.

One by one the rattles were silenced and the snakes slowly crawled into the rocks. When Webb was sure he could move without fear, he retraced his steps along the trail and made his way back to his horse.

With his long-sought treasure deep in his pocket, and the treasure of a deeper understanding in his heart, he turned his horse homeward, well away from the green and gold of springtime in the Wichita Mountains.

The Kiamichi Bigfoot

Kiamichi Country covers a vast area of southeastern Oklahoma. Both the Kiamichi Mountain range and the river of the same name cross through the heartlands of the Choctaw Nation. Large-scale timber operations and tourism rule the economic landscape. But deep in the wilderness, where few people dare to live, the woods are the sovereign domain of black bears, panthers, and something much more frightening.

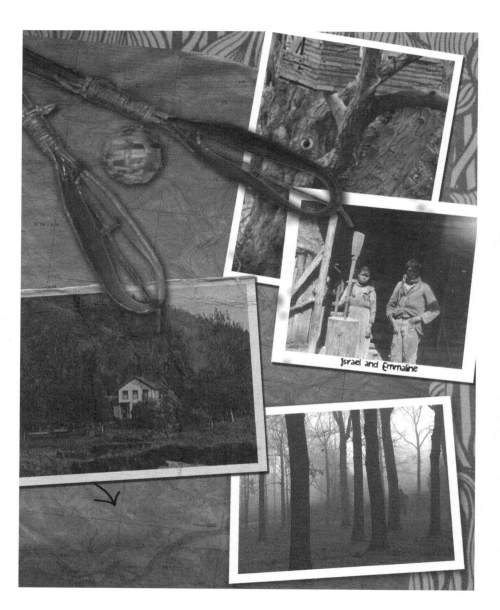

In all of his ten and a half years of living, Israel Anowatubbi had never felt so angry. Everyone was much too fond of giving him orders, and now, of all things, he was being blamed for something he didn't do.

Israel's family home was a typical Choctaw clapboard house of four rooms nestled deep in a wooded valley of the Kiamichi Mountains. He lived with his parents, older brother, and two younger sisters.

But now, there would be one less in the house. Israel was running away. With only a flashlight, a pocket knife, a rolled up blanket, and a bagful of beef jerky, he left the cleared grounds of the farm and walked into the surrounding trees. He looked back. Sadness filled his thoughts.

I wonder if I will ever see them again. He would miss his mom for sure and she would miss him, too, he figured. *But the rest of them will only miss me 'cause they won't get to boss me around.*

Along the banks of the Little River, several other Choctaw families had settled, most of them more than a hundred years earlier. After returning from the First World War, his father and two uncles had built the farm from nothing.

Life on the farm was hard work. There were plenty of chores, like tilling the soil, planting seeds, harvesting the crops, and feeding the animals. Israel didn't mind the work. But he sure didn't like people always telling him what to do. He probably should obey his mother and father, he figured, and his uncles, too. They were his elders and he respected them. But lately, it seemed that everyone thought they could order him around: his older brother Simon, his cousins Edward and Flora, even his two little sisters, Emmaline and Abigail. They all took their turn.

The real trouble started when Israel didn't get water for the night's washing. It was his chore to get two bucketfuls of clean water from the river every day before dark.

He was out in the pasture practicing stickball when he looked to the sky and realized it was already near dark. He raced home to get the water buckets, but nighttime had already settled across the farm. He looked down the dark path that twisted through the trees to the river. He was scared. He feared both the dark woods and the trouble to come for not getting the water.

Walking into the kitchen, where his mother was making dumplings, he stood holding the empty buckets. She shook her head. No explanation or excuses mattered.

"*Hushi?*" he said. *Mother.* "I forgot and now it's too dark."

"Aw 'right," she sighed. "But just this one time, Israel. You're old enough not to forget." She took the bubbling broth from the cook stove using her apron as a potholder, .

"*Kil-ia,*" she muttered. *Let's go.*

They had walked the river trail so often that the darkness posed no real problems. Israel raced ahead of his mother, never getting too far away. They each filled their own buckets and carried them up the hill.

Behind him, Israel could hear his mother's breathing grow deeper and more strained. It sounded like grunting. He turned back to make sure she was okay.

His mother stood unmoving in the trail, her finger to her lips. She was not breathing heavily at all. From the trees came a piercing grunt-growl-moan.

"*Ba-li-li*!" cried his mother. *Run!*

Without another thought, Israel ran as fast as he could. He held on to the bucket of water, knowing if he dropped it he would have to come back and get it later.

He flew along the trail until he reached the back porch, then turned to look behind him. His mother was nowhere to be seen. He dropped the bucket and screamed, "Mama!"

"Right here, son," came her voice from behind. She was standing on the porch. Somehow she had passed him unseen.

"What was that?" he asked.

"I don't know," she responded, trying to catch her breath. "But it was big."

Israel dumped what was left of his bucket into the water barrel. His mother had dropped hers on the trail. "I'll have Simon go get it in the morning," she said, putting her arm around Israel and leading him into the house.

Among the glowing lamps of the supper table, the family gathered for their meal of chicken and dumplings. Between large spoonfuls, Israel's father looked first to his wife and then to Israel. "You two alright?" he asked.

"We're fine," said Israel's mother. "Just got a fright."

"That's why you get the water before dark, Son."

The look on his father's face relaxed. "There's nothin' out there to worry about, you know. Us Choctaws have always been friends with the animals, even the ones that growl in the dark. Long as we let them have their homes, they will do the same."

"Simon," said his mother, "I need you to go get that bucket I dropped. First thing in the morning." Israel's older brother nodded and shot him a quick look that said, "you're dead meat."

Then Israel's father sealed his doom. "Israel, you go with him. And make two trips to fill the barrel all the way up." It was useless to argue. No one argued with Israel's father, not even his uncles.

Come morning, before it was light outside, Israel filled the water barrel by himself, hoping his brother would leave him alone. When all his other chores were finished, he left the farm and went to his secret hiding place.

Years ago, Israel's two older cousins had built a tree house out of old barn planks. One day, without their knowledge, Israel had followed them. But now they were away in the army and the tree house was all his. Israel took great precautions to never leave a trail that anyone could follow--especially not Simon.

Later that afternoon, Israel returned home. His father, brother, and two uncles were looking at the ground near the water barrel which was lying on its side covered in mud.

"That's one mighty-sized footprint," said Uncle George.

"Biggest I ever saw," said his father.

"Maybe's not from a man," added Uncle Push. "Maybe's *Iyi Chitto*." *Bigfoot*.

Simon pointed to Israel and said, "Maybe he turned it over and made the giant footprint in the mud. He's mad 'cause of last night. He's trying to trick us."

Israel's father looked his way and motioned him forward.

"It wasn't me, Poppa. I filled it up this morning, all by myself."

"I thought I told you to help your brother do it."

"I got up real early and did it myself, so maybe he wouldn't be mad."

"You let me worry about your brother being mad. Now, what do you s'pose happened to this barrel?"

"I don't know, Poppa. Maybe Bigfoot, like you said."

"Nevermind," his father said. "You get this barrel cleaned up and filled again before supper."

"But it wasn't my…"

His father's angry look made him swallow the rest of his words. "Yes, sir," was all that came out.

From there the day got worse. It took two trips to the river just to get enough water to clean the barrel and four more trips to fill it again. On the last trip, Simon was waiting for him.

"I outta knock the barrel over so you have to do it all again."

"You better not," said Israel.

Simon took a step toward Israel and punched him in the arm.

"That's what you get for sneaking off this morning." Then Simon ran off toward the hog pens.

Israel went into the house, rubbing his arm, and sat at the table.

His mother walked in behind him. "Get out of my kitchen with those muddy feet," she hollered. "If you got nothing better to do, go get me some squash from the garden."

I shoulda stayed at the tree house, he thought. *In fact, I should just stay there all the time.* That's when Israel decided he would run away.

The boards of the tree house creaked every time Israel rolled over. It had been dark for several hours and he was having a hard time getting to sleep. Already he regretted not bringing his pillow. His arm was cramped from laying his head on it. He missed his bed. If he weren't so afraid of the dark woods at night, he would already have gone home. But if he we went back now, they wouldn't be worried, only mad.

The wind picked up and the trees outside rustled more violently. Suddenly, Israel realized it was not all the trees, but just one. He grabbed his light and crawled to the wall nearest his feet. Peeking through a cut-out hole in the planks, he saw the single tree shaking back and forth in the moonlight. Someone was down there.

"I know it's you, Simon," he shouted, lighting the base of the tree with a flick of the button.

At first, he saw no one. Then a giant, earth-colored hand emerged from behind the tree trunk, followed by a monstrous head covered in hair.

The giant, man-shaped hairy thing again shook the tree until Israel was sure it would be pulled loose from the ground. The monster grunted ferociously. *Iyi Chitto*, he thought.

Israel ducked beneath the tree house window, but as he did, the flashlight caught on the board and fell from his grip to the ground twenty feet below. He heard the thump! as it hit. He looked through the cracks in the floor. The light had gone out and the forest below was completely black. Israel huddled against the wall, afraid to move.

For several hours he waited in the dark, listening for any sounds of the beast. Finally convinced *Iyi Chitto* was gone, Israel climbed down from the tree house. He lowered his back and carefully looked in all directions as he crept toward home.

Half-way there, he thought he heard heavy footfalls in the darkness behind him. Then he heard the most dreadful sound ever: UH-REEEKK-KK.

He ran. Like a deer, hopping fallen trees and dodging vines and underbrush, he ran. The crashing sounds behind confirmed his fear. The beast was after him. Looking over his shoulder, he turned forward again, just in time to see the low-hanging tree branch that knocked him unconscious.

Israel's eye-lids fluttered as the blurry world around him gradually took shape again. It was early morning and he was on the porch. *Not my porch*, he realized. *Uncle George's porch*. He sat up and rubbed the swollen knot on his forehead.

The front door opened and he heard a squeal of delight. It was his cousin Flora. "Poppa," she shouted. "He's here. It's Israel."

His uncle came to the porch and knelt to his side. "Goodness, boy! Do you know how much craziness you caused? We been searching for you all night."

"Well, at least you're safe now," said Uncle George, picking Israel up. "Let's get you home. Your folks are gonna be so happy you're safe."

When Uncle George brought Israel home, his mother cried tears of joy. His father hugged him close, and even Simon apologized for being so mean.

Israel said nothing about *Iyi Chitto* or the night's harrowing escape. But all day he wondered how he had gotten to Uncle George's porch.

At supper that evening, Simon came to the table. "Uncle George gave me this to give to you," he said to Israel. "He said it was on the porch next to you this morning." Simon handed his younger brother the broken flashlight. Nobody but Israel noticed that the mud wrapped around the handle came from a handprint three times bigger than a man's.

Later that night, Isreal lay in bed. He fluffed his pillow and thought how good it was to be home. Replaying the events of the last few days in his mind, he realized his father was right. The animals were friends of the Choctaws--even *Iyi Chitto*, the Kiamichi Bigfoot.

The Red River Monster Fish

Oklahoma is a land of lakes and rivers. Beginning in the Panhandle of Texas, the Red River flows southeast, the primary border between the two states, and eventually empties into the mighty Mississippi River. Surrounding the various waterways of Oklahoma are small towns populated by folks who love a good fish story. As each one of these stories gets bigger, so do the fish. Though most are exaggerations, every once in awhile someone will pull a monster fish from the dark waters, and a legend is born.

The Worst Fishermen Ever

"It used to be so peaceful being on the river at night," started Raymond Wilkerson. "But now, with them kids gone missing, it's kinda spooky, and it seems darker out here."

"Ray! Will you please be quiet. You're gonna scare off all the fish."

"Well, hand me some of that stinkbait and I won't have to keep talking."

"Get it yourself, it's right there."

"Dang, Robert, you're closer, just hand it to me."

"If I am closer, it can't be by more than a foot. So get it yourself."

Still angry that after 53 years his brother did not abide by the Whoever's Closer Rule, Ray reached across the boat for the small tub of ground chicken liver and other assorted smelly globs of goop. He was probably the only person in the whole world that actually liked the smell of stinkbait. It reminded him of his childhood and fishing with their Pappy. "Everybody knows that the closer person has to do the other one the favor," he muttered.

Raymond and Robert Wilkerson were notorious along the Red River as being the worst fisherman ever. The two old brothers spent more time arguing with each other than actually doing any real fishing. But they tried…and tried. Rod and reel, jugline, trotline, trolling – just about anyway they could to land the biggest fish. Yes sir, they had tried it all. They even tried noodling once, an Oklahoma tradition of sticking your hand underwater and into the mouth of a catfish, or at least you hope it's a catfish. But that's another story.

The Wilkerson brothers sat beneath the star-filled sky in a small aluminum boat, their fishing poles hanging over the edge. Robert kept the fishing net ready in his other hand--just in case.

"Hey Ray, hand me one of them sodas, will ya?"

Because he was closer to the ice chest and *did* follow the rules, Raymond reached toward his brother with the icy can. A sudden loud splash behind the boat made him jump and the soda can flew through the air and into the river.

"What was that?" he whispered.

"I dunno, but it was big. Real big."

"Get the spotlight."

Long, slow arcs of light swept across the murky surface. Nothing moved. No sound except the slapping of waves against the boat.

"Over there," Raymond pointed.

The light swung around. The brothers froze. Two big, red eyes glistened behind a long row of white dagger-teeth. A huge scaly head lifted above the water and slammed into the side of the boat. Robert, who had stood to get a better look, was nearly thrown overboard.

"Was that a…" began Robert.

Raymond nodded. "Alligator gar."

Their eyes widened in terror. "It couldn't have been," continued Robert. "Not that big. It was twice as big as me and I'm six-one…and them teeth…did you see them teeth?"

Again Raymond nodded, his jaw gone slack.

The next morning, over scrambled eggs and coffee at the bait shop breakfast bar, Raymond recalled the previous night's adventure. "I'm telling you, Pete, it was a durned ol' alligator gar that tried to knock us out of our boat and eat us. It was more'n twelve feet long with the biggest teeth you ever seen and red eyes glowing like the devil."

"Save yer fish stories for the outta town folks, Ray. I been fishin' the river here as long as anyone and I know better."

"But what about them disappearing kids? Maybe it's this gar that's getting them."

"Raymond! Quit it. There ain't no twelve-foot alligator gar in the river. It's the current that's sweeping them kids away, or maybe quicksand, but it sure ain't some monster fish with devil eyes."

Raymond and Pete had been friends a long time. But now he had his doubts. If Pete didn't believe them, who would? The answer was *no one*.

"We gotta go prove we ain't crazy," Raymond told his brother later.

"Goin' after that gar will only prove that we are crazy," said Robert. "You seen its eyes."

"Our honor is at stake."

"Honor *schmonor*…our lives are at stake."

"Just think what folks'll say if we bring in a fish that nobody believes is possible. And the kids it's been havin' for dinner? We can be heroes for getting the monster that's been eatin' them kids."

Robert stared at his brother for a long time. "Aw'right. But I'm bringing a speargun…and my shotgun…and…"

"What shotgun?" asked Raymond.

"My new one I'm fixin' ta buy today…and I'm bringing a big knife…and dynamite…yeah…I'm bringing dynamite too."

"Fine. Bring whatever you want."

"Oh, and Robert?"

"What Raymond?"

"We're gonna need a bigger boat."

Late that night, as the moonlight danced on the rippling surface of the river, Raymond and Robert navigated their boat in a wide circle where they had seen the fish several nights past. Each brother cast an ever-watchful eye, looking for any sign of the monster.

"Raymond, quit belly-achin'. If we coulda found a bigger boat, we'd a-brought it. Now keep looking."

"And I didn't know where to get any dynamite."

The muffled quiet of the river surrounded them. They listened for any sound of splashing. They watched for any sign of movement. The hours crawled by, marked by the slow descent of the moon above. Raymond stood at the bow, holding his shotgun at the ready. Robert held the spotlight, scanning the surface.

"I got a stomach ache," whispered Raymond. "Must've been all them sodas I drank."

"Here," said his brother, "have an Alka-Seltzer."

Robert reached to hand his brother the plastic bottle and Raymond leaned toward him.

KER-SPLASH!

The boat lurched sideways, violently launching Robert into the water. The spotlight created the luminescent ring as it sank beneath the current and followed Raymond's brand new shotgun to the bottom of the river. In the newfound darkness, Raymond scurried to his knees and hollered.

"Robert! Where are you?"

He looked over the side of the boat and squinted, pushing his face forward as he tried to focus in the dark. Sweat rolled down his brow, stinging his eyes.

"Rob-ert," Raymond called over the waters, leaning out as far as he could.

The boat lurched again. The sudden shift knocked Raymond to the floor. The back of the boat lifted higher as something big crawled in the boat with him. His fingers found the handle of a wooden paddle. He lifted the paddle in front of him and slowly turned.

"Don't just sit there. Help me in," his brother demanded in an angry voice.

"Robert, you scared me. I thought you was a goner. I thought the monster fish got you."

Raymond grabbed his brother by the shirt collar and pulled. Their scrunched, red faces were only inches apart as he struggled to get the soaking-wet Robert in the boat.

WHAM!

Once again, Raymond was thrown to the floor. Robert's arms were pinned to his side and he couldn't move. His legs hung, flailing, over the side of the boat. He began to scream. So did Raymond.

Less than six inches from their faces was a long row of huge, gnashing teeth. The monster fish was in their boat. Robert was helplessly trapped and Raymond was paralyzed by fear.

"Do something!" shouted Robert.

Raymond just kept on screaming.

"Raymond! Do *something*!"

Raymond came to himself and bolted into action. He shoved the paddle in the monster's gaping jaws. With his other hand, he reached for the bottle of Alka-Seltzer and dumped the white disks down the blade of the paddle into the gar's oversized mouth. Then he grabbed a can of soda pop and emptied it chug-a-lug style down the fish's throat.

The humongous fish, weighing nearly five hundred pounds, thrashed in resistance, flipping the boat over. The two brothers splashed and hollered out for each other. Robert swam toward Raymond and they held onto each other in the quiet darkness.

But only for a moment.

"Here it comes again!" screamed Robert. The monster's red eyes reflected moonlight as the fish came closer.

A loud *POP!* sounded from deep inside the fish and the eyes disappeared below the surface of the water. A moment later the fish resurfaced and rolled slowly over till its pale underbelly bobbed on the waves of the river. White, foamy fizz bubbled from the gills.

"Must've been the Alka-Seltzer and soda pop. I always heard if you mixed the two that it could blow up yer stomach, but I always figured it was just an urban myth."

The brothers swam to the boat and grabbed the rope tied to the bow. They looped the rope around the fish's tail and swam, dragging both boat and monster fish to shore.

The next day, word spread all along the river about Robert and Raymond Wilkerson's gigantic alligator gar. Local police looked into Raymond's theory about the missing children. They discovered the stories were all just rumors. At first, Ray was quite upset that he had been duped by the hoax. But during the investigations, it was revealed that a few weeks back he had overheard Deputy Beams tell Pete that he was out looking for Mrs. Gilder's missing *kitties*. Ray thought he had said *kiddies* and told everyone who would listen. Ray was no longer all that angry when it became obvious that he had started the rumors in the first place.

So, sadly, the Wilkerson brothers were not recognized as valiant saviors of children. But they did get their picture on the front page of the local newspaper. And they did look quite heroic standing on either side of the huge fish hanging from a chain. It was reported that the two brothers giggled like candy-coated schoolboys when they read the headline -- THE RED RIVER'S GREATEST FISHERMEN CATCH MONSTER FISH!

The Witch of Kitchen Lake

Accursed and haunted places lurk near most every town and city. Down dark dead end streets and along lonely highways sit any number of houses associated with mystery and spookiness. Several miles east of Moore, Oklahoma, was once such a house. Now, there are only the remains of an old chimney in the middle of a field near Kitchen Lake. But the stories from around there tell of both a haunting and a curse. It's certainly, no place to be found after dark. And whatever you do, don't provoke the witch.

A rising plume of thin black smoke caught the eye of Betty Lynn Peterson as she stood at her sink washing dishes. Through the small kitchen window, peering past her own reflection of gray hair and wrinkles, she saw the smoke in the distance. The rising tendrils brought back painful memories of a dark and destructive fire. Every few years, the smoke returned, serving as a reminder to folks nearby of that awful day, so long ago. Blackening an otherwise clear blue sky, it rose from the old rock Chimney – all that remained of the house – where once lived the witch of Kitchen Lake.

From the other side of the room, she heard the whine of the metal spring stretching across the screen door, followed by the clack-clack-clack of wood slapping on doorframe. That sound grated on her last nerve. She turned to tongue-lash the culprit, when…

"Grandma Betty!" shouted her grandson. "The smoke! It's there again!"

"I see it, Bobby. No need to rip the back door off its hinges."

"Sorry, Grandma," said Bobby, with his head lowered. Betty Lynn had to smile. *Boys will be boys*, she reminded herself.

"Is it the witch?" he asked. "Is she come back to get us all?"

"Of course not, Bobby. She died a long time ago and she can't come back." *At least, I hope not*, she thought.

"C'mon, Grandma. I heard all about it. I know everything. How when you was a kid, that old woman was making everyone get sick and how Great-Grandpa George and them other men went after her."

"Hush, Bobby. Like I said, that was a long time ago. Great-Grandpa George had nothing to do with burning that house. Now leave it alone.

Some things are best forgotten." The words rang false in her ears. Some memories, no matter how hard you try, can never go away.

"Aw' right, if you say so," mumbled Bobby, turning on his heels and darting outside, leaving streaks of mud on the freshly mopped floor.

"Robert Eugene Peterson!" Betty Lynn scolded. But the boy was gone. She poured herself another cup of coffee and sat down at the table, remembering it all.

"He's so sick," Mrs. Naismith cried. "My baby boy is so sick."

"We'll get him to the doctor," Mr. Naismith assured her. "Betty Lynn, go get the truck and pull it around front." Betty Lynn was so scared she was crying, but once behind the wheel, she wiped her eyes, started the engine, and eased the truck from beside the barn to the front gravel driveway.

On the way to the doctor's, Betty Lynn rode on the rotted boards in the rusty bed of the '43 Chevrolet. The truck bounced along the dirt roads and past the lake before turning onto the newly paved highway towards town. The ride was much smoother now and the whir of rubber on asphalt made Betty Lynn sleepy. She watched the blurry roadside shoot along behind the truck.

As they passed the wood-planked home of Old Lady Weller, Betty Lynn saw a bright bonfire in front of the strange woman's house. The dancing flames, reaching higher than a man is tall, licked the deep-blue darkness of the night air. The light from the blaze illuminated the front of the house in a warm amber glow.

The old woman was also bathed in firelight. Her arms were stretched high, tossing large bundles into the fire. Each time she did, sparks were sent to the heavens, and as the bundles burst into flame, thick green smoke choked the starry sky.

It was a strange sight to see for a young girl. If Betty Lynn had not heard so many horrible stories about Old Lady Weller, she might have watched the sparks with amazement and wonder. Instead, she wrapped her arms around her knees and buried her head, scared of the woman and the tales of her mysterious powers.

When they reached the home of Doc Sprague, Betty Lynn saw at least a dozen cars and trucks parked in the yard. Several men stood talking in small circles on the front porch. Others were sitting off to themselves, their worried faces resting in their hands.

Betty Lynn's father stomped the brakes and the old truck's tires slid on the gravel. He jumped from the cab and ran to her mother's side. Flinging the door open, he snatched up the bundle of blankets that held their baby boy. The covers lifted from the baby's head and Betty Lynn saw her brother's face. It was brick-clay red and spotted with dark sores.

The Naismiths waited outside for several hours. Eight neighboring families also lingered while their own sick children lay inside the doctor's house. Mrs. Sprague circled through the crowd offering lemonade and words of comfort.

"Don't worry, dear. Your brother will be fine," she said, patting Betty Lynn on the shoulder. But her words seemed hollow and her voice quivered.

Fearful questions floated among the gathered. Is it an epidemic? Is it contagious? Then another word crept along in the darkness, whispered from man to man, carrying with it a new level of fear – witchcraft.

The small circles of people in Doc Sprague's yard grew into a large one. "It's gotta be her!" Andy Danforth shouted. "She's the one making our kids sick."

"I ain't standing for this no more," hollered Bill Price.

Betty Lynn knew these people. They were parents of her friends and schoolmates. Around town they were always friendly. But now they were angry and fierce.

"On the way over here, I seen her doing her magic. Building a big fire for conjuring spells, and such. Right out front of her place," said Beckett Jones.

Then Bill Price cried, "Let's go get her! Who's with me?"

Sixteen men shouted back with frenzied acceptance.

They hopped into four cars and drove away. Betty Lynn was glad her father was not one of them. She looked up at him and he put his arm around her, saying, "There's no chance I'm leaving your mother or your brother now. They need us here with them. Besides, there's no telling what men like that'll do when they're all worked up. I s'pose they're just worried and scared, same as the rest of us, but it ain't gonna be good. I seen it too many times. It ain't never good when men go off in a mob with so much anger."

Eight year-old Bobby Peterson loved his grandmother dearly, but she could be so secretive. *If I ever wanna know about the smoke, I guess I gotta go find out for myself.* Hopping onto his bicycle, he leaned over the handlebars and pedaled hard. He rode along the red clay road till he came to the highway. Lines of tar-filled cracks splattered the paved surface and part of the game, for Bobby, was to zip back and forth between the potholes, like a slalom skier in the Olympics.

Bobby reached his destination. He had been forbidden by his grandmother to ever come to this place. But now, he sat on his bicycle looking across the open field. In the center, surrounded by tall grass and heaps of rubble, was the rock chimney. Wisps of black spirals rose with elegant grace. Watching the smoke slither and writhe in the breeze was hypnotic and Bobby was drawn to it. Bobby wanted to see what was burning. What's causing the smoke? He dropped his bike and hiked through the grass. Sticktights clung to his socks. They scratched his legs, but he kept moving, closer to the mouth of the fireplace.

Betty Lynn was standing on the porch with her father when the front door opened. Doc Sprague led her mother by the elbow and in her arms, wrapped in a new blanket, was her baby brother. The question in her father's eye was answered before he had a chance to speak.

"It's gonna take a few days to know for sure, but I think he's gonna be okay. I tended his sores and gave him some medicine to help him sleep. But I have to be honest, I haven't seen a sickness like this. Ever. So I can't be certain of anything right now."

On the ride home, Betty Lynn sat with her back against the cab and sharp winds swirled, whipping her hair across her face. She felt the truck slowing to a halt and turned to see why. A nightmare unfolded before her.

Old Lady Weller's house was a roaring inferno. Her yard was full of cars. As men stood watching, large roof timbers collapsed and giant flames shot from the windows. Betty Lynn searched the fire-lit faces. Old Lady Weller was no where to be seen.

Betty Lynn's father stepped from the truck. "Stay where you are!" he hollered back to his daughter. Then he turned his attention to the men.

"What have you done?" he shouted. "Tell me that woman is not in that house!"

No one moved.

"Bill? What's going on here?"

"We had to, Frank…she was killing our kids."

"Andy? I know you got more sense than this. What happened?"

"I dunno, Frank. We just came to scare her is all. But when we got here, she started screaming curses and talking crazy. She said she was putting an evil spell on us and our families. Then she ran inside. We threw burning logs through the windows to smoke her out. We just wanted her gone, Frank. But she never came out."

Without warning, the back end of the house exploded. Splinters, flames, and burning embers flew in all directions. The men hit the ground, covering their heads. Betty Lynn dove deeper into the bed of the truck. She could hear bits of wood and rock falling around her.

In the cab of the truck her brother shrieked and broke into a prolonged fit of coughing. Betty Lynn started crying. She was just as scared of the old witch as everyone else, but the thought of the woman burning seemed so horrible.

When it appeared safe enough, she lifted her head and peered over the side. Most of the flames were blasted out by the explosion. The men slowly stood, removing splinters of wood and brushing small sparks from their jackets. Nothing of the house remained--except for the rock chimney.

Through the cab window, Betty Lynn saw her mother lifting the blanket from her brother's face. He was no longer crying. His eyes blinked like a butterfly's wings and he made a sound of gurgling joy. Stretching his little arms, he fell asleep.

"I'm taking my family home. I'll be back," she heard her father say. Betty Lynn resettled against the cab. A small piece of rock near her foot caught her attention. It sparkled blue in the moonlight. Scratched deep into the surface of the polished stone was a strange symbol – a raindrop, or maybe a teardrop. Putting the stone in her jacket pocket, she looked to the night sky. Smoke still billowed from the chimney. Against the darker backdrop, the rising spirals took on a greenish hue.

Bobby strained his neck to see inside the fireplace opening. He could see the glow of something burning on the blackened walls, but nothing of the fire itself. He crawled through the charred piles of rubble until he saw the flames. The burning object inside was oddly shaped and looked alive. It seemed to move in the flames, writhing in the intense heat.

Bobby could already feel the heat against his cheekbones. He moved closer. The oily shapeless glob twisted once again. Now, less than two feet from the burning source, Bobby squinted and leaned even closer.

CRACKKK!

The fire sputtered and spit green sparks in Bobby's direction. He fell back into a pile of rubble, helpless and in pain. The burning on his face was unbearable. He felt the fire in his chest and his lungs gave forth a long shrieking scream. As he looked to the sky, he saw the thin black smoke grow thicker and turn green. A final moan escaped from his throat. His eyes slid shut. Only darkness remained.

The strange appearance of the black smoke always made Betty Lynn a little nervous. It carried with it so many troublesome memories. She dumped the last few drops of her coffee in the sink. It had been more than an hour since Bobby had burst through the kitchen door. Betty Lynn began to worry. *Maybe he's riding his bike,* she thought. *But he always tells me when he's leaving.*

She looked toward the smoke. It was thicker and greener. Intuition told her where Bobby was. Betty Lynn ignored her aching knees as she ran back the house for two things – her car keys and the blue stone she had kept all these years.

Betty Lynn's car skidded to a halt in the gravel on the side of the highway. Lying among the weeds, the chrome handlebars of Bobby's bike glinted in the sunlight. Pulling herself from the car, she called out.

"Bobby?"

With urgency, she shuffle-skipped through the tall grass and carefully stepped over the rocks and charred boards of the old woman's burnt-down home. Searching the piles for any sign of Bobby, she paid no attention to the sticktights that covered her long cotton skirt.

Turning toward the chimney, Betty Lynn saw her grandson lying unconscious on the ground. She ran to his side and lifted his face in her hands.

"Bobby? Can you hear me? Talk to me."

She lifted her head to the opening. "What have you done," she screamed at the burning green flame.

The sparks crackled higher and brighter. A strange hissing came from the unnatural blaze.

Betty Lynn returned her attention to the boy. His face was red and blistering, pox-like sores dotted his forehead and neck. Betty Lynn had seen this same sickness so long ago, on her brother. He had lived--barely. But it was clear that her grandson was dying.

Reaching in her shirt pocket, she clutched the stone and raised her hands. Her lips trembled as she mumbled words of prayer.

The green flame responded to Betty Lynn's plea with a roar of hot wind spiraling from the top of the chimney.

"Please!" Betty shouted. "Release him. We did nothing."

The sky darkened and strong bursts of sweeping air blew dirt in her face. Thick black clouds formed above and crackling thunder ripped the sky.

On her knees, leaning into the wind, she screamed her words even louder.

"We did nothing to you! I cried when you died!"

The darkened world around her grew brighter as the rush of air fueled the green flame. The intense heat was now unbearable. She fell to the ground next to Bobby. Rolling over to shield him, she fought for air. She was choking.

Next to her, Bobby coughed in unison.

"We did nothing," she repeated, lifting a heavy arm and tossing the stone into the flames. Her head sank to the ground. Betty Lynn looked to her grandson and with her last breath, she whispered, "I love you, Bobby."

Then her eyes closed.

Loud, booming thunder shook the ground. With jilting force, cool air came rushing back into Betty Lynn's lungs. The edge of a rock dug against her cheekbone and she opened her eyes. With considerable effort, she sat up, rubbed her face, and looked around. A heavy rain was pouring from the sky. Then she remembered where she was and why.

The smoke was gone and only a small trail of steam rose from the fireplace as the last of the green glow flickered and then blinked into nothingness. Bobby was still lying next to his grandmother, his breathing returned to normal.

The downpour soaked their hair and clothes, but that mattered little. For Betty Lynn, it was a cleansing rain – the kind that washes a person's soul.

Bobby stirred. She lifted his head to her lap and leaned forward, wiping the water from his face and kissing his forehead. The sores and burning redness were gone. He opened his eyes, slowly.

"I love you too, Grandma."

Author's Notes

The eight stories in this collection were all based to varying degrees on existing Oklahoma legends and oral recollections. As is often the case with legends, the facts, as they are reported, often supercede the narrative. Character and plot are minimal and lack the tension of a well-written fictional piece. Additionally, descriptive passages often fall short of the great potential to develop a setting that pulls readers into the story-world.

It was my intent to take the essence of the legends and craft them into full-blown stories with all the ghastly images, troublesome situations, and spooky delights that captures the imagination of young readers. It was also my intent to light the fire of student interest in Oklahoma history, geography, and culture, or better said, the people, past, and places that make our great state unique.

I would like to comment on the use of dialect. My purpose here is to give an authentic voice to characters representing real Oklahomans: people who carved homes out of the prairies, mountains, and bottomlands of our state. My paternal grandmother was the daughter of German and Irish immigrants, the other of Polish descent. One grandfather was Scotch-English and the other Choctaw-Chickasaw. Like most Oklahomans, my ancestors came to this "land we belong to" along the Trail of Tears, in covered wagons, or steam ships from across the ocean. They came seeking new beginnings; carrying even older traditions, beliefs, and stories.

The roots of these stories are largely from the passed-down oral tradition of simple tellings. In many cases, they are combinations of multiple tales woven together. For instance, The Kiamichi Bigfoot *contains elements of several stories told to me by Choctaw elder Buck Wade – stories of his own childhood.*

Deadman's Treasure *combines two archetypical stories that thrive in southwest Oklahoma, buried treasure tales and rattlesnake stories.*

The primary impetus for The Ghost of Mingo Creek *was a selection from the WPA oral history project of the 1930's and can be found in the Oklahoma History Center archives. The source of* Jimmie the Doodlebug *originated from the* Oklahoma Folklore Collection, *housed at the Metropolitan Library System's downtown branch.*

The Boy Who Cried Lion *found its way into the book from stories my dad tells of his own childhood experiences as a paperboy. And, while* Mr. Apple's Grave *does actually exist, the legend rose from several generations of Ardmorites spreading stories of strange adventures. Only they really know if these stories are true. Every lakeside bait and tackle shop has photos and legends of their own local* Monster Fish, *but listener beware, the stories are certain to grow each time you hear them.*

Finally, while these stories are meant to entertain and enlighten, they also teach us not be greedy, prideful, mean, or just too curious, as in the case of The Witch of Kitchen Lake. *The aforementioned tale also includes a chilling warning against mob psychology, of following the crowd.*

The Ghost of Mingo Creek and other Spooky Oklahoma Legends *is a work of fiction and should be considered a collection of short stories based on legends, rather than the actual legends themselves. In story and character development, artistic liberties were certainly taken to enhance the reader's involvement. It's been great fun for me to creep and crawl through the darker landscapes of Oklahoma legends, gathering and retelling these stories. It is now up to you the reader to continue on this harrowing journey through the Sooner State's most mysterious haunts and hideouts. Enjoy, but heed the ghostly warnings and beware of beastly growls in the dark. You just never know…*

A Note About the Photographs

The photographic compositions found in this book were created to lend an authenticity to these stories based on Oklahoma legends. While these photographs depict actual people and places, they are meant only as graphic representations of the characters and events in the stories and do not suggest that the subjects of the photographs are in any way related to the characters and events in the stories in real life.

The majority of the photographs came from the Library of Congress, Prints & Photographs Division, FSA-OWI Collection. Credit for the photo of the Choctaw children: Grant Foreman, Grant Foreman Collection, Courtesy of the Oklahoma Historical Society [8470.55] The amazing alligator gar is included thanks to the kindness of Bill Meyer at the Gar Anglers' Sporting Society. Finally, Greg Rodgers and I owe a debt to our family members - living and dead - for making appearances in the photos.

All characters appearing in this work are fictitious. Any resemblance to real persons, living or dead, is purely coincidental.

Larry Johnson
Forty-Sixth Star Press

About the Author

Greg Rodgers is a storyteller and writer in the Oklahoma City area. He is a member of the Choctaw Nation of Oklahoma and often tells traditional and contemporary Choctaw stories at schools, libraries, festivals, and tribal events throughout the country.

Greg is also an accomplished Native American flute player. His story performances are often enhanced with the addition of flute music, traditional songs and chants, as well as the steady rhythmic beat of his deerskin hand drum.

As a writer, Rodgers has published a short-story, "Harriet's Burden," in the 2006 Nov/Dec issue of *Storytelling Magazine*. His adapted short-story "Giddy Up Wolfy!" is among the many wonderful American Indian trickster tales included in the forthcoming graphic anthology *Trickster*.

In a perfect blend of symbiotic pursuits, Greg strives to weave his enthusiasm for storytelling, folklore, and oral history collection into one seamless effort to preserve and perpetuate the cultural landscapes of both Oklahoma and the Choctaw Nation.

CHEROKEE HIGH SCHOOL LIBRARY